BARNABY'S CUCKOO CLOCK

Written and illustrated
by
RENE CLOKE

AWARD PUBLICATIONS
LONDON

10655766

The tiny shop among the roots of the oak tree in Hopping Wood belonged to Barnaby and Bertha Bunny.

Barnaby picked up a letter from the mat one morning and read it as he sat at breakfast in the room behind the shop.

"Dear me!" he said. "Here is a letter from my Aunt Brown-paws. She is coming to see us today and will arrive on the bus at three o'clock."

"She will want to hear the cuckoo clock she gave us for a wedding present six years ago," said Bertha, "and it hasn't 'cuckoo-ed' since young Flip put the cuckoo in the bath."

"It wouldn't float at all," grumbled Flip.

"She will be very annoyed," said Barnaby. "I wonder if I can get it mended before she comes."

He took the clock from the wall and looked at it. It was a pretty clock, with acorns and flowers carved in wood around its painted blue face.

"I'll take it along to old Prickles and see if he can mend it," said Barnaby. The clock was heavy, so he put it in a wheelbarrow and trundled off to find Prickles.

Old Prickles, the hedgehog, looked at the clock and rubbed his head because he was puzzled.

"The clock is working," he said, "but the little bird doesn't jump out."

"I can mend watches and clocks and also clean them. I can even make new springs, but making little birds pop in and out and say 'cuckoo!' is a thing I never learned to do. It doesn't seem natural to me."

Meanwhile, Bertha Bunny was very busy. She took some flour, currants, butter, sugar and a large pot of raspberry jam from the shelf in her shop.

She also took a loaf of bread and a pot of paste for sandwiches.

"Now, Flip and Flop," Bertha told her two young bunnies, "you must mind the shop while I make some cakes and jam tarts for Aunt Brown-paws' tea. Be polite to the customers and keep the shop tidy."

She got out her rolling pin and pastry board and set to work.

Flip and Flop thought it was great fun serving the customers. They popped extra sweets into the bags for their friends, Dumpling, the black piglet and Merry, the kitten, from Hopping Wood Farm.

"I want some very tall candles," said Flipperty Frog, "you know, the sort that will stand well out of the water in my dining room."

Hazel and Tufty Squirrel had come to buy a checked tablecloth and Flop had to climb the stepladder to get one from the shelf.

The stepladder wobbled and down fell poor Flop straight into a barrel full of apples.

"Help!" shouted the little rabbit as the barrel tipped over and all the apples were scattered about the floor.

Dumpling pulled Flop up to his feet.

Larry, the puppy, and Merry collected the apples. Then, everyone had a glass of lemonade, to help them to recover from the shock of it all.

Dumpling had a biscuit as well, because he said the accident had made him feel quite weak.

Barnaby walked slowly home with the cuckoo clock that wouldn't 'cuckoo'.

"Aunt Brown-paws will think we have been very careless with her present," he kept muttering. Then, as he pushed the wheelbarrow along through the wood, a voice called out to him . . .

"Hullo, Barnaby! Taking your clock for a ride?"

Down from the branches of a thorn tree hopped
Charley Cuckoo and his friend Willie Wren.

Barnaby told them about the clock.

"The works are all right," he explained, "but the
bird doesn't 'cuckoo' when it pops out."

Charley looked very wise.
"I have an idea," he said.
"I will crouch on top of
the clock and call 'cuckoo!'
at the right time and Willie
will pop out in place of the
little wooden bird. I'm sure
your Aunt Brown-paws won't
know the difference."

"Splendid!" cried Barnaby and they all hurried
along to tell Bertha about the grand plan.

Bertha wasn't too sure about the grand plan.
"It might work," she told them, "but Aunt Brown-paws will be very cross if she finds out."

"If the bus arrives at three o'clock and she leaves by the last bus at a quarter past four, we shall have to do it only once," said Willie.

"If you can do it without being discovered, I will give you each a jam tart," said Bertha.

So, they all bustled about and tidied the burrow which was their home.

Flip and Flop laid the lace table cloth and Bertha brought out her best tea set. She put all the tarts and cakes she had made upon the table.

Barnaby hung the clock high up on the wall so that Charley couldn't be seen sitting on the top. Willie crept inside the clock and closed the little door.

"Now!" cried Flip, who wanted to practise. "It's just on three o'clock."

Out popped Willie.

Charlie Cuckoo cried: "Cuckoo! Cuckoo! Cuckoo!"

Willie popped back inside the clock and closed the little wooden door. "That was wonderful!" exclaimed Barnaby, full of admiration.

Aunt Brown-paws arrived a few minutes later. She was a very stately old rabbit and everyone felt a bit afraid of her grand manner.

"Well," she said as she looked at the cuckoo clock on the wall, "I'm glad to see that the wedding present I gave you is keeping such good time. I shall look forward to hearing it at four o'clock.

I must leave you at four to catch the last bus,"
Aunt Brown-paws added. Flop giggled and pushed
Flip, who tumbled over and nearly tripped up
Bertha as she carried in the teapot.

Barnaby pretended that the little bunnies were
trying to show Aunt Brown-paws some tricks and so
they both turned somersaults and stood on their
heads. Aunt Brown-paws looked a bit surprised and
said she thought the burrow was too small
for games like that.

Then, Aunt Brown-paws poked her whiskers into Bertha's shop and said that it wasn't kept very tidily. Of course, there had been no time to tidy up after Flop's adventure with the apples.

"Come and have tea," said Bertha before Aunt Brown-paws had time to find fault with anything else.

So, they all sat down.
Bertha worried
about whether she
had remembered to put
sugar in the cakes and
whether there was
enough jam in the tarts.

But she need not
have worried. Aunt
Brown-paws was
enjoying her tea.

She ate four pieces of bread and butter, three sandwiches, two slices of currant cake and a jam tart.

"Do have another jam tart," said Barnaby politely. Aunt Brown-paws looked at the two tarts that were left on the table.

"They do taste good!" she said. "Perhaps I . . ."
Aunt Brown-paws was interrupted.
"Cuckoo! Cuckoo! Cuckoo! Cuckoo!"
They all jumped and looked up at the clock.
Aunt Brown-paws was so pleased to see
Willy Wren pop out
that she didn't notice
that the hands were
pointing to ten minutes
before four o'clock.

"Four o'clock!" she cried. "I must catch the bus. Goodbye, my dears, and thank-you, Bertha, for such a lovely tea."

"I am glad the clock is in such good order, Barnaby," she called out. "The note of the cuckoo is very strong and clear."

Aunt Brown-paws was away to catch the bus.

Out came Willie from inside the clock and down flew Charley Cuckoo.

"Why did you ' cuckoo!' so early?" asked Barnaby. "It was only ten-to-four. You could have spoiled everything for us."

"Your aunt was just going to take another jam tart," said Charley in a cross voice, "and the two that are left are for us!"